I0766350

BOOK TWO OF THE LIRTLE™ SERIES

GRAY'S QUEST

UNDER THE SILVER MOON

WRITTEN BY: JULIA D. KYTE

INSIGHT PROVIDED BY: CAMERON LANDIES

ILLUSTRATED BY: K. MICHELLE EDGE

Lirtle Inc.
www.lirtle.com

FOR

ALECIO, TRISTAN & RIVER

BOOK TWO OF THE **LIRTLE**™ SERIES

GRAY'S QUEST – UNDER THE SILVER MOON

Paperback ISBN: 978-1-7368876-3-9
Hardcopy ISBN: 978-1-7368876-4-6

Julia D. Kyte (Self-Published)

South Jordan, UT

With Special Thanks To: Randall B. Bateman, Esq., Randi Godoy, Cason Adams, Cassi Horrocks, Kyle Canham, Kayla Faurot, and of course, my family.

Lirtle Inc.
www.lirtle.com

LIRTLE™**:** Noun

A heroic and tiny imaginary creature,

possessing magical qualities, with physical

features most akin to those of a lion cub and

a small turtle.

TABLE OF CONTENTS

*T*HE PROLOGUE

Under the blue moon of Book One, back at the bottom of the ravine below the Snakadactyle lair, and just off the dirt path on Pangolin Mountain, the lirtle children finally are reunited with their friend and brother at last...

"Samuel." Lev quickly pulled himself up and hurried over to the greatly weakened but now smiling Samuel.

"Lev, am I glad to see you! But what are you doing here, and is that Gray?" Samuel's grin was a mile long, but his disbelief was clear.

"Yep, it's a long story and I'll tell it to you ... when we get you out of here!" Lev joked back delightfully, as he was bombarded by an ecstatic Saw who was flitting around between them both.

"Saw, yes, I know. It's Samuel! Yes, we will get him out of here. Just a second." Lev pushed off the little owl, and at that point Gray was moving. When he saw his brother, with an enthusiasm that probably did more harm than good, Gray leaped onto and wrapped his arms around Samuel as he yelled: "Samuel, you are alive! I'm so happy you are alive!" At which point, the strain just became too much, and Gray broke down into a blubbering, crying, sweet, little brother mess as he clung to his older brother as if his life depended on it. The others shushed him, knowing the Snakadactyles were sleeping but could awake at any moment.

"Gray - it's okay, Gray. We got him, Gray." Dawn gently peeled off the pile of mush from Samuel's shoulder that was now Gray and looked at the rocks that were trapping Samuel's leg.

"Come on everyone. We need to move these rocks if we want Samuel to come home with us." Dawn started applying pressure on the various rocks, testing each one, until she finally found the weak link that she wanted. With a ferocious growl, she put her shoulder into it and pushed the rock back until Samuel could pull his leg away. As Samuel tried to move, he was so weak, he just fell forward. His tall, athletic frame was luckily caught by Violet, Dawn, and Lev, as well as Gray to some extent as he just grabbed on to his brother's torso and hugged him for dear life.

Between the four of them, they managed to walk/drag Samuel with them as they walked doggedly back up the dirt path. Staggering, they kept going until they got to right before the drop. There, they found an alternating zigzag path which led them back up and out of the ravine, finally, and into the rolling hills at the edge of their valley home that they knew so well.

...

As the four young lirtle children helped

Samuel along, who they knew would be okay, Lev and his little gang stood at the edge of the rolling hill. In the silhouette of the full blue moon as it slowly set before the dawn, they knew they had made it. They were going home! With fists raised in success, the young band of heroes started down the hill that now glowed again with moonflowers and minerals, a small owl happily dancing around their heads, and the Rainbow River gurgled off in the distance – the land of the lirtles was saved.

The *Lave* lirtles were returning home victorious ... and a new era had begun.

$\mathcal{P}$ART ONE – THE SNOWFALL

Gray wiggled happily just a little bit as he stuck his feet into his snowshoes. It had been the best few months. Ever since they got home and they were presented by the Bright Birds to the whole town as the group that saved the land of the lirtles, and rescued his older brother, Samuel, they had been treated like heroes.

It had been great. Gray got treats for days, and there was a whole dinner in their honor at the end of the Blue Moon Festival. He even got to sit at the head table, and no one called him baby Gray any longer.

But the best part of the whole adventure had been that finally, once they got back to the village, that he was allowed to play with the other lirtle kids - if he was back by dark, his grandmother let him stay out for hours, it was glorious.

Gray shivered as he stepped outside. He was delighted with the early snow, but it was much sooner than it had ever come before as it was only late fall. The wind was brisk, such that Gray was thankful for the fur on his body and the shell on his back. He started trekking quickly because the large snowflakes were already making it difficult to see and he only had a few hours to play with Lev and his friends, who were waiting for him by the hill.

The gang was all there with their snowshoes on, while some of the other lirtle children were sliding down the hill on their backs, using their shells like sleds and having a blast.

Gray gave a quick hi five to Dawn and Violet before falling in behind Lev. They were going on an adventure to see if they could trek to the magical glen they found last year, as they were all dying to know if the snow would melt there or not.

It was only a twenty to thirty-minute journey to the glen. Since everything was flattened down by the snow, it was much faster snowshoeing than in the summer when they had to wade through all the long green grass.

All of the children were plenty warm by the time they found the glen again. As they stepped into the hidden meadow, a hush settled over them. While it was covered in white, the snow was not falling there, and everything sparkled brilliantly as the water gurgled from the stream into the lunar pools. The moonflower at the other end rose serenely in a brilliant burst of white and blue. Entranced by its beauty, and excited to examine the distinct mark on its leaves that Lev, and the other children now knew was that of the *Lave* lirtles, an emblem that some of them bore − those three rushed over to the flower, while Gray dawdled behind.

Gray picked up a pretty, smooth stone beside

one of the lunar pools, and he skipped the stone and watched it settle. As it drifted down, suddenly the rock disappeared and Gray's eyes widened as smoke swirled in the pools again. Then the smoke cleared to show the Bright Birds, with Alrik and Stelios, but in a different lirtle village on the other side of Pangolin Mountain.

Gray leaned forward as he was drawn into the scene unfolding …

"You must help us." The pretty woman lirtle pled to Alrik with tears in her eyes and the male lirtle stood beside her with his head bowed.

Alrik shook his head solemnly as he, the leader of the Bright Birds, stood with his wings crossed serenely. Stelios (the secret protector of the children), stood beside him, with a few of the other Bright Birds standing nearby, serious, and quiet, as large snowflakes swirled and fell onto their shoulders.

"The Hyarks killed our only son, and you cannot expect us to now send our daughter to cross the Highlands and be ripped apart. She is too young, she is …" the woman's voice trailed away as she buried her head in her hands. But as she went to turn away, she threw her hands out as if to try and catch the whirlwind that blew past her.

"No, Ailne!" The man and woman both cried

out, even while knowing they could not stop her.

The beautiful lirtle child hurtled towards Alrik and then, with a dancer's grace, paused, before bowing upon one knee before him. Alrik smiled, despite the dire circumstances. Ailne looked up and at Alrik. Although small in stature, her silky, silver blue fur only highlighted her stunning crystal eyes framed by a delicate sheath of armor, and she presented as the perfect warrior child.

"I am ready Alrik, I will take the moonflowers to the Batterflies. I will avenge my brother."

Alrik gently raised the girl up by her shoulders. He stepped aside and both looked towards the beautiful iridescent moonflowers that glowed in what looked like another magical glen behind Alrik, where no snow fell.

"You are such a warrior, young Ailne and you remind me so much of some other brave lirtles who also had to go on a quest to help save the land of the lirtles recently. But you Ailne, you cannot do this alone, in three nights time or by the full moon, the moonflower must get to the Batterflies before the snow becomes too deep and the Batterflies hibernate, or they will die, and they are the key... all will be lost if ...

####

"GRAY! Gray, what are you looking at!" On snowshoes, Violet had silently come back and startled Gray, such that he almost fell headfirst into the lunar pools before he caught himself.

"Violet - Did you see her, did you see Alrik, or Stelios, did you see the other glen? Violet - they are in trouble, the other lirtle village! They need our help from the Hyarks on the Highlands!" Gray was talking so loudly, and fast to Violet while pointing at the water, that the other lirtle children came back over to see what the commotion was all about.

"What are you talking about Gray, there is nothing there?" Violet said as she stared into the water. Gray stopped talking to look down at the water. Sure enough, it was just a clear pool of water, so when Lev and the others joined them, they only saw themselves, a bunch of young lirtles, (albeit special ones since they had recently discovered that they were all either *Chosen* or *Lave* lirtles) flushed from the cold in the pool's reflection.

"Come on Gray, it's starting to get dark, so we better head back before your grandmother starts to worry or decides you can't play with us again." Lev tugged at Gray's hand before he and Dawn and Violet all started traipsing out of the glen and back into the falling snow, where the wind was creating drifts as dusk set in.

Gray took one last look at the water and wondered if he had just imagined what he saw, before he turned away and hustled to catch up with the others who were already disappearing into the swirling white.

…

Later that night, all warm and cozy in his bed, Gray stared up at the ceiling. He could not get the girl's crystal eyes out of his mind. She was the most interesting lirtle child he had ever seen, and he wanted to help her, as well as her parents. Gray remembered when he had thought his older brother, Samuel, had been hurt, or even killed by the Snakadactyles, and he had been so afraid. She … her name was Ailne… Gray said her name softly to himself, had certainly not seemed afraid like he had been to face their mortal enemies, the Hyarks. No, she had seemed determined to take them on. Yet, Alrik's words kept ringing through Gray's head: "… Ailne, you cannot do this alone."

Gray sat up in his bed. He knew what he needed to do. He needed to go help her, to help the other lirtle village. Even if the others didn't believe him, he knew what he saw.

Quietly, so as not to wake his grandmother, Gray slipped out from his covers and went to the chest at the foot of his bed. He took out the cape that his brother left for him before the first quest. Then he took out the magical blanket that was light as a feather. The Bright Birds had given Lev and the gang each one of these blankets which protected them during the day from being seen. Gray kept digging and found his pouch that he could put across his chest where he tucked the blanket into, along with some snacks that he kept stashed under his bed for special occasions. Finally, he took out the wooden staff he had, since he could not go get his snowshoes because they were drying in the front room close to his grandmother's bedroom - who would surely wake up if he made so much as a peep.

"All set." Gray whispered to himself. He pushed open the slatted cover on his window and started to pull himself out. His breathe sucked in as the wind and snow hit his face full force. The snow had picked up in the last couple of hours. As Gray slid over the ledge, he fell into the bank below with a swoosh. And he lay there for a second, grateful for the thick layer of powdery snow that made for an easier landing than the last time he had snuck out a few months ago. Still, he could not quite ignore the worried hoots of the little owls that were huddled together on the ledge under the overhang.

"It's okay guys, I have got to go help her, but I will be back in a jiffy." Gray called out over his shoulder.

And with that, Gray started off into the night, and the soft snowflakes quickly blurred his figure from sight.

$\mathcal{P}$ART TWO – THE DISCOVERY

"Lev! LEV! Have you seen Gray?"

Lev groggily rubbed his eyes and wondered if he was dreaming, but then he heard it again – muffled yelling from outside: ... "LEV!!!" 

Lev, rolled out of bed and walked over to his window, where he opened the slats and saw that Samuel stood outside on the path that wandered close to his house.

Samuel waited, in snow that came past his knees with snowflakes still twirling all around, while Lev tried to open his window cover that was blocked by snow. Finally, Lev pushed the cover open.

"Have you seen Gray?" Samuel asked again, and worry could be heard in his voice.

"No, I have not seen him since yesterday when we dropped him off at your grandmother's house after snowshoeing, just around dusk. Why, what is up?"

"Early this morning, my grandmother woke up because it was unusually cold in the house. So she went into Gray's room, and the window was partially open so snow had blown in everywhere. She saw that while Gray's snowshoes were still at the front door, his chest in his room was pretty much empty."

"What do you mean, pretty much empty?" Lev asked the question even as his stomach took an unsteady drop.

"His cape, pouch, and blanket were gone, and my grandmother said that he had a wooden stick in there that was gone, and all the treats that he normally tried to hide under his bed were gone. She thinks Gray has left for a trip, but she doesn't know where or why, and she is worried sick." Samuel had started pacing as he was talking.

"I think I know who may know where Gray has gone. Let me get dressed and let's go talk to Violet, give me a minute." And Lev shut the window cover and left Samuel outside to worry (even more than his grandmother was), about where his little brother had taken off to.

#####

Gray's legs felt like dead weights as he trudged through the snow. He had set off last night and had thought he was making progress, but as the snowstorm worsened, it had slowed him down. The slice of the moon that he knew was above him, had been blocked by the cloud cover. And while light, when the wind pushed the snow into swirling clouds, Gray could not see and he had been only able to move in the smallest increments because he could not risk stopping off the rocky path. It was the only path that would lead him beside Rainbow River, and around Pangolin Mountain into the rough lands that he and the rest of the gang had only talked about.

Yet, Gray had not realized just how rough the lands would be that he was entering. Hours ago, any familiar trees or landmarks had disappeared. The shadow of Pangolin Mountain loomed scarily over him from the left, and now even Rainbow River that meandered on his right, no longer looked like water that Gray recognized. It had changed from a sparkling, multi-colored happy stream, to a dark and brooding body of water, where eerie animals and fish swam in or by it.

In fact, Gray had only been able to stay on the path that was now hidden by deep snow, by walking beside the black, swirling water, and following the orange orbs of lights, that were almost iridescent, as they floated in the depths of the river. Gray knew that he was following the deadly Foxfish. The Foxfish were predators, with teeth like piranhas, smooth scales, and bushy foxlike tails. But, at night, their iridescent scales glowed orange, like a beacon or a warning as they swam with the river, so one could safely stay away. During the day, however, their scales blended with the river bottom they swam above, so they were virtually undetectable until some unsuspecting deer or animal stepped into the water, and the Foxfish moved in a flash to bite their prey.

Gray tried not to let his imagination run wild as he imagined those poor animals. He realized he had started shivering though. In the last few hours the cold and the sheer weight of the snow clinging to his fur was pulling Gray down, and slowly a bit of fear was creeping into Gray. As maybe, maybe he was a bit too far away from home. Maybe, he should have thought this through a bit more. Whimpering, Gray noticed a few boulders off to the side of the path and saw a fallen tree lying beside it, where he thought there was a tiny spot of dry rock that had not been covered by snow. Gray stumbled on hidden rocks on the path, almost falling into the river, but he wedged his staff quickly and stopped his fall. Breathing a sigh of relief as the orange orbs that had risen in a flash, sank back down into the depths, he pushed back and walked the few steps to the small crevice he thought he saw. He crawled between the boulder and found indeed, that if he wedged himself down, the fallen tree provided enough cover that he was able to get out of the storm.

Although it was still nighttime, and Gray knew he could not travel during the day because it was too dangerous, Gray told himself he would just sleep for a few hours because he was just so tired. Gray pulled out the little blanket from his pouch and smoothed it over him. Gray thought he must be more tired than he thought, because suddenly it felt like it was fluffier than any blanket he had ever felt. It was so warm, he felt like he was lying beside his grandmother's hearth at home. And in as long as it took for him to pull the blanket over his body and up to his eyes, Gray's head slumped down and he fell into the deepest sleep ... where even in dreams, he dreamt of Ailne's crystal eyes.

#####

Samuel leaned against a wall, just shaking his head. Violet, Dawn and Lev all sat on the floor in the front room of Violet's parents' home, where a fire cheerily cackled in the stone chimney. Samuel didn't feel the warmth as Violet sheepishly explained what had happened the day before.

"You're positive that he said the other lirtle village and that the Hyarks were attacking them on the highlands?" Samuel asked in disbelief. He still could not believe that his little brother, who was only six years old, may have taken off by himself, around Pangolin Mangolin, where he would have to trek away from the protected lands and into the wild and rough terrain before getting to the other lirtle village. A village that was just below the Highlands and near the swamplands where the Hyarks had been banished to, so long ago. With the plan to get there in only two and half days or by the time the full moon rose.

"It makes sense as the other lirtle village and their warrior lirtles take the moonflowers from their protected glen up to the Batterflies before they hibernate at the first snowfall. The Batterflies need the moonflowers to allow them to survive those months when they go into the deep recesses of the mountain, or else they will die. Without

Batterflies to pollenate the land, come spring, nothing will grow, and our land would turn to dust." Dawn spoke in her firm and knowing way.

"And Gray mentioned a girl, and that the Hyarks were attacking them?" Samuel asked wearily.

"Yes, I am sorry Samuel, I didn't believe him, and I would never have thought that he was going to go try and help them... by himself." Violet scuffed her feet along the floor miserably.

"It's okay Violet, you didn't know. It makes sense now though; the tracks are barely visible with the amount of snow that has fallen but they lead off towards the path around Pangolin Mountain. I am going to go after him." Samuel was already preparing in his head what he needed to pack, and so tuned out for a second the voices of the others, but suddenly it came back loud and clear. "We are coming with you." Lev said it and the other two were shaking their heads, nodding in agreement.

"We faced the Hyarks together last time, and Gray is going to need our help if he is going to try to take on more than one this time. His strength is impressive, but he is so young he won't know how to control it. Our powers are stronger together." Lev spoke and while Samuel started to protest, he took one look at the faces of the other three lirtles, all *Lave* lirtles (meaning lion brave) and realized it was pointless.

"Fine. We go back and tell our families what we are doing and then we meet back here in one hour to go get Gray and help the other lirtle villagers if we can." Samuel looked around, and it was decided.

And with that, the group dispersed back out into the winter wonderland.

PART THREE – THE BITE

Gray groaned as his eyes fluttered open and he started to stretch his limbs, which were now pinned under a carpet of heavy snow. He paused as he realized it was still daylight and  he stopped moving. Gray cautiously peered out to make sure that he could not see any Snakadactyles flying above or around him. He saw that the snow had stopped falling and by the placement of the sun in the sky, he figured it was late afternoon. Gray did not see anything flying that may want to eat him, so he slowly eased himself out from his snow cocoon. As soon as he stood up and into the open air, the frigid temperature made Gray wrap his cloak around his body as much as he could. He thought he would just get a few hours of a jump start on the trek in the daylight since he was awake and didn't want to waste any more time.

Gray plodded through the snow, wondering if it was ever going to end. The path had started to go upwards, and the rocks and edges were getting larger and harder to navigate as he kept falling over rocks that he couldn't see. He could hear a slow hum in the distance, and he realized that it must be the waterfall near Lucky's Ledge, which meant he was almost to the other side. He was trying to speed up as he started to see the path curving and he looked up and saw the beautiful mists for the waterfall ahead. As the sun started to go down, he paused before stepping forward, because he thought he saw Lev's pet miniature owl, Saw, fly up over the lip and hover above the waterfall. Gray reached up a hand to block the sun's rays as he was confused since Saw would have been coming from the wrong direction. Yet, in that second, Gray felt his foot slip off a rock and as he tried to regain his balance, he knew he was too close to the river and his right foot dipped before stepping down into the water. He felt the words "Noooo," rise onto his lips in the same moment that he saw the dark shape race to the surface. Gray tried not to scream like a baby as he saw the Foxfish's head break the surface, teeth bared, and bite down onto his ankle. With one small paw, he reached down and grabbed the fish, ripping it off easily as he threw it down the river probably thirty feet in one herculean throw.

Gray stepped back onto the path and was so irritated at himself. He knew better then to be out in the daylight, he should have been paying better attention. Although the bite was small, when he put weight onto his foot, Gray realized that he could barely walk, the damage had been done, and there was blood starting to trickle down his fur as he limped down the path towards the waterfall. Gray was cursing at himself as he hobbled along. He could not believe he had been so clumsy. And now he was all alone with no one to help. How would he ever get there in time? It was about to be the start of the second night and now, he was hurt badly, and he would not be able to keep walking for much longer. Gray kept fighting to stay upright but the one hundred yards to the waterfall took all his strength. Already he felt feverish and knew the bite was likely getting infected. The roar of the waterfall was so loud now, and Gray could feel the fine spray as he walked beside the water. Gray thought he was delirious as he fell to his knees. He just was going to rest a bit. He paused and for a moment, he felt warm as the snow swirled above him. He was just going to close his eyes for a second. As his lashes closed, Gray started to daydream about snowflakes touching down on his cheeks so suddenly, it felt like a soft slapping across his face.

Slap, slap, slap, slap, slap.

Gray's eyes fluttered open, and a little ball of brown fuzz with big eyes stared into his.

"Saw." Gray struggled to stay conscious, as the tiny brown owl used his beak and pinched Gray's ear. "It was you." Gray's eyes closed again.

"Owwww." Gray's senses suddenly sharpened as the pain from the owl's peak ran through like a pint-sized lightning bolt.

"Okay, I am up, I am up." Gray stumbled to his feet. Saw kept pulling on his ear, and Gray took the last bit of his strength to follow Saw as Saw pulled him towards the waterfall.

As Gray staggered again, he realized he was at a spot where the path went up, on almost a natural rock staircase beside the waterfall, there was a small trail that led off the path and seemed to pass behind the waterfall.

Wincing in pain, Gray knew he could not climb up the rock staircase and so with Saw pulling him, he stepped onto the small trail and wondered whether he was about to fall and likely not get to see his friends again as the Foxfish would get him. Gray paused, held his breathe, he stepped and...

Gray went through the freezing ice-cold mountain water and rolled into a large and eerily quiet space behind the waterfall. He felt like he was in another world. As the fever set in, Gray smiled as it was a pretty blend of colors behind the water as they streamed through and the fading rays of sunset poured in like a sunbeam... and Saw was there, buzzing around him in a worried frenzy. Gray just turned to his side, before he smiled at Saw, and passed out. But this time, Gray did not dream of the warrior child with crystal eyes. This time, Gray's dreams were a haphazard blend of sunset colors, mixed with Saw, and then Stelios, a Bright Bird who helped them before, and then a large white creature he had never seen before, with a pouch and some little creatures inside it.

$\mathcal{P}$ART FOUR – THE SLIVER

"Gray, Gray, wake up dear Gray." A sing song voice, soft and melodic, stuttered near his ear. So familiar, and comforting. "Gray, Gray, wake up, I am here to help you."

Gray moaned and slowly opened his eyes to see a friend. "Holly." He whispered.

"Yes, I am here." Gray looked up and Holly, their dear friend, the Pangolin who had shown them how to get to the top of Pangolin Mountain, was kneeling beside him, smiling, and blushing so prettily beneath her long, long lashes. She gently wiped his face with a warm cloth. Saw sat nearby on a stone, watching intently. Gray gingerly moved his leg and winced, but the pain did not feel as badly as it did before. He looked down and saw that his ankle had been wrapped with what looked like paper-thin strips of bark and there was a thick salve under it.

"Holly, you are the best." Gray smiled, and as soon as he spoke, Saw flew over to land on his shoulder. "I'm okay, Saw."

"Holly, how did you get here?" Gray's voice was still weak.

"Well, when Saw found me yesterday, he was

in such a state over you, Gray, going out in the snowstorm alone, that he just told me ... ummm, Holly stammered suddenly, "ummm, rather, he tugged at me, I mean, owls can't talk right, right. Yes, anyway, I figured out that I needed to find you and then he raced back off into the storm. And I could not have gotten here with the amount of snow that was falling but my friend, Baran Bunroo, had been visiting with my family as it had been a while. He was kind enough to bring me here, right after you came in, just as the sun was setting, and we have been here visiting with Saw and waiting for you to wake up since then."

Holly was flushed again by the time she finished talking, and as she gestured daintily to the corner of the landing, Gray saw the most interesting large creature sitting but in an upright position. Gray realized with a start, that it was the creature from his dreams. A white figure with the upper body of a bunny rabbit, and big, graceful ears, a soft looking tummy in the middle, with what appeared to be a full pouch, that sat on long fluffy feet or haunches, like a kangaroo.

Gray sat up on his elbows, and gingerly wiggled his foot, and was surprised that it seemed to be feeling better by the second. He sat up and looked at Holly, she giggled shyly and looked down. "My family our healers, and my Nona gave me the salve on your ankle, as well as some other things, when I did not know exactly what was wrong. In about another twenty minutes you should be right as rain and able to walk, although if Baran has room, I would strongly suggest that we ask if he will let us catch a ride with him back to the Highlands and the other lirtle village."

"The Highlands and the other lirtle village — you know where that is?" Gray stood up with that and stared at the creature he now knew was Baran.

Before Gray could figure out if Baran understood him or not, Holly answered his question.

"Yes, the Bunroos live in the Highlands and when the first snow falls, they turn white to blend in with their surroundings, but in the summer, their fur returns to tan or light brown."

"Well, Mr. Baran the Bunroo, if it is possible ..." Gray scratched his head as he realized he did not know how long he had slept and if he was already too late.

As if reading his mind, Holly said quietly, "it's still the middle of the night, if we go now, we can get there by dawn and you can go plan during the day with Ailne to figure out how to help the other Lirtles, before the third night, and the full moon."

With hope revived, Gray turned then to Baran the Bunroo, and politely asked, "May we please go with you." And with a regal nod of his head, Baran indicated that yes, they could and with his paws, gently held open the pouch as a clear invitation to get in.

Slowly, still testing out and not quite believing that his foot was a hundred percent better already, Gray walked slowly over to Baran, but not before Holly rolled over and then quickly climbed in. She popped up and batted her long eyelashes at Gray, "okay, just gently come in to, but be careful, we have another traveler, who apparently snuck along for the ride." Inquisitively, Gray peered into the pouch before he pulled himself in. And he started to yelp, before he caught himself when he saw it was just a little, white ball of fluff staring back at him with bright green eyes.

"This is Bastian, Baran's youngest son." Holly made the introductions, and the green-eyed fluff ball grinned at Gray. Gray finally pulled himself into the pouch and found two little arms wrapped around him in a hug. Gray hugged Bastian back as he suddenly felt extremely tired again - cozily wrapped up in the pouch with friends, both new and old. Gray did not even realize that the silence was not due to the protected surroundings – but rather had instead occurred because the water was no longer running outside. Over the last four hours, the temperature had dropped so low, that the waterfall and Rainbow River had frozen solid. Gray's eyes started to close as the rhythmic bounds of the Bunroo lulling him back to sleep. Gray remained blissfully unaware that outside there was almost five feet of snow, or that his brother, Samuel, and his friends were struggling to catch up behind him ...

*P*ART FIVE – THE HALF

The cave behind the waterfall had long been empty when the four other lirtle children struggled past the huge icicles, and wall of ice, before collapsing into a heap together on the dry floor. They were so tired, they did not even notice the first rays of dawn that danced through and made kaleidoscope rainbows all over the walls.

With teeth chattering, Dawn reached into her backpack and grabbed the magical blankets that she had been carrying for the group. She handed one to each of them. As Dawn did so, each blanket evolved into the softest and thickest gray material she had ever seen, matching the floor of the cave perfectly. Without so much as a word, Lev and Violet grabbed their blankets, and made little delighted gasps as they sank into them. After the tense hours of trudging and fighting through drifts of snow (that were so deep that, but for Samuel's fierce determination, they may have all turned around instead of going forward), the heavy protection from the elements felt blissful.

Making sure that Samuel had his blanket, Dawn finally wrapped hers around her own body. She decided that the Bright Birds were amazing. It felt like she was sleeping on the softest bed ever, and the warmth – ooohhh, with a little sigh, Dawn smiled, then was sound asleep within seconds.

$\mathcal{P}$ART SIX   THE THREE-QUARTERS ROUND

It was the lack of movement that woke Gray up. He realized that neither Bastian nor Holly were in the pouch with him. Then the delightful smells hit his nose and started it twitching. Gray waited a minute to stretch before he poked his head out and took in the new but still familiar scene before him.

He saw some villagers sitting with wooden mugs of the traditional lirtle drink – a yummy, apple-based brew that was laced with cinnamon, oranges, and honey. It filled the room with a homey smell, and he saw them eating something that he couldn't quite see but it smelled great. And then, he finally saw her. She was sitting by her family at the stone table in the middle of the room, although small, her presence seemed to fill the room. She all but sparkled as she sat. He breathed in her name .... Ailne.

Gray did not get a chance to think anything more about her though as some tiny ancient lirtles, sitting on the benches with Ailne's family, were in a loud discussion with the other lirtle villagers and Ailne's father. The discussion was getting heated. Gray looked up and saw out one of the windows, that it looked like it was the morning as he saw a low sun to the east, so he knew he had a bit of time. Gray looked around the room and instinctively ducked back down when he realized that in addition to Baran the BunRoo, there were several other large Bunroos in the room, making it far more crowded than he realized. And the Bunroos towered over the others and while silent, their presence was clearly felt. Luckily, the Bunroos were also focused on the group around the table, and no one seemed to notice that he was awake.

Gray stared as one of the ancient lirtles, a tiny lirtle with a pale, sea foam green shell, and a flowing mane that fell over his shoulders, stood up on the table, all twelve inches of him. And, while likely well over one hundred years old, when he clapped his paws together, it was loud enough to make everyone fall silent.

His voice shook with wisdom, still strong though, as he continued the statement he had been making to the group:

"We saw the vision, and the vision showed Ailne on the highlands fighting the Hyarks with the Bunroos but she was not alone ... there was another lirtle, a *Chosen* lirtle, around her age with her at the start and there were *Lave* lirtles that came from afar – she did not fight the battle alone. We must wait for these other lirtles to come. If you try to fight them now, more lirtles will be lost. You must wait."

Loud gggeeffffaaawws and defiance were

heard around the table, as the adult males shook their heads negatively at the statement.

"Another child is going to fight with Ailne? We are supposed to rely on children to protect us and the land of the lirtles from certain demise if we fail to get past the Hyarks? That is ridiculous." The lirtle villager spoke loudly in disbelief from beside the table, and others shook their heads in agreement.

"We should go now and try to attack them when they are not expecting it." The same villager continued with many others joining in agreement.

The ancient elder just shook his head at the noise and stated again: "No, we must wait for..."

"Me. I think you are all waiting for me." Gray's voice cracked on the last word and all eyes turned towards him. Gray could even feel Baran's gaze drop down to his own pouch quickly.

As the stares continued, Gray squirmed uncomfortably before he steeled himself and slid out of the pouch. He walked over to the table where Ailne and the others sat and climbed up onto the end of one of the benches.

"What did you say?" The outspoken villager spoke once more.

"I saw the vision from the lunar pools on the other side of Pangolin Mountain. I dreamt of fighting with Ailne, and I am one of the lirtles that recently went up the Mountain to clear Rainbow River and saved the land of the lirtles. I am the *Chosen* lirtle that fights with Ailne in the vision."

Gray looked around expectedly to see nods of approval or acceptance. Instead, he felt his little hackles rising on the back of his neck as suddenly, loud bellows of laughter started out of one villager, and then another, until everyone was laughing at him.

Gray felt heat in his cheeks and knew they were turning red from embarrassment at being laughed at, even as his small body tensed with anger.

"I AM the *Chosen* lirtle that was sent to help you and I can prove it!!" Gray moved without thinking, hopping off the bench, and then he lifted the entire table using only his two paws – with the ancient tiny lirtle still standing upon it.

"SEE!!!" Gray was yelling as he stared at the faces of the villagers around him and was mortified to feel the tears starting to roll out of his eyes, even as he stood with the table above him.

"We believe you Gray. It's okay." The quiet, solemn voice commanded the room. Now all heads turned as Stelios walked out of the shadowed corner.

"Gray, please put your elder, and the table

down. And please do so slowly...," Stelios said it calmly and kept his eyes on Gray's eyes, ignoring the fact that Gray was blinking furiously to try and stop the tears. Stelios was pleased when Gray started to shake his head no, but, as if coming to his senses, he paused, and then Gray carefully lowered the table back down to the floor, without damage to the table or to the little ancient lirtle who looked startled but unharmed.

"Okay then, well, that is settled." Stelios briskly clapped his wings together. "Folks, I think Gray here and Ailne need to spend some time today and this afternoon to start planning on how they are going to take on the Hyarks tonight, and we are going to leave them alone to do so. I further, strongly recommend that you all listen to what these two have to say, and if they ask for your help, you give it to them, is that clear?"

Stelios gazed around at the still mostly astonished faces of the other lirtle villagers. Slowly, some stood up and others sheepishly looked down from the steely stare of the majestic creature - whom all of the villagers knew was one of the Bright Birds, the Seers that helped protect and guide the lirtles throughout time.

"Everyone now, let's get going, except Baran. Baran, I would like you to be available to Gray and Ailne around lunchtime today, along with a couple of your most trusted comrades. I believe once those two start discussing a plan, your help will become quite invaluable, does that work for you?"

Gray looked over to see Baran the Bunroo give a quick nod of his head, and almost bow before he then quietly hopped out the door with his other silent friends.

And, just as quickly, everyone else left, including Ailne's mother and father, who looked at Gray distrustfully as they walked out of their own home. Despite Stelios and the ancient lirtle's words of support for the two lirtle children, to the adult lirtles that were at the meeting, there was great doubt that these two lirtles were going to be able to come up with some kind of a master plan to defeat the Hyarks and get the moonflowers to the Batterflies, in only a few short hours.

Stelios himself, turned to face the two youngest lirtles. He wondered what they would be able to accomplish in such a short time, for while the Bright Birds could see what happened in the land of the lirtles, they could not entirely stop or change the outcomes, no matter how much they may have wanted to. Stelios was particularly worried knowing the events as they related to Gray, but even though he was troubled with what was to come, Stelios was only allowed to offer a small word of encouragement to Gray and Ailne before he too, had to go.

"We believe in you, and that you both can do this." Stelio looked down on the two sets of wide eyes looking at him, and he placed a gentle wing on each shoulder. "Remember, you are stronger together." And with that, he too, stepped out the door and firmly pulled the wooden slab closed behind him.

...

There was nothing but silence for a minute as both children just looked at each other. Besides how pretty her eyes were, Gray noticed the sun beams coming through the window of almost mid-day and the dust motes settling back down after being stirred up by all the villagers.

Given Gray's admiration of Ailne, it surprised him when she spoke, and instead of the friendly overtures he had imagined in his mind during his trek over the last two days, instead, he heard nothing but a snotty attitude.

"I don't need your help; I can do this alone." Ailne stomped her foot as she said the words. She blew a piece of silver blue mane that had slipped out of her braid from her eye.

"I am the one that lost my brother, not you. I need to avenge his death, and you are just going to get in my way. Besides, you are just a baby." She sniffed as she said the last part, which immediately triggered Gray again.

"I. Am. Not. A. Baby." Gray said slowly, with anger flaring his nostrils as they started twitching.

"Oh yah, fine, on the count of three, we are both going to say our ages and whoever is older, gets to send the other one away – deal?" Ailne felt confident that she was going to win this bet.

"On the count of three then, we will say our ages, okay?" Again, Gray nodded to Ailne.

"Okay, one, two, three ….." And with that both children yelled out at the same time …

"Six."

"I am six."

Ailne sank down on the bench table, as if the air had been knocked out of her, as she responded with a defeated, "Nooooo."

"Ha!" Gray grinned for the first time in what felt like ages, "I told you so."

"Okay, fine. We will rock, rabbit, lizard it, then, and whoever wins that, can send the other one home, deal?" Ailne refused to give up.

"Deal." Gray eagerly balled up his paw and placed it on the flat of his other palm.

"Rock, rabbit, lizard, shoot." They both chanted together, and each flashed out the two fingered rabbit.

"Best 2 of 3." Ailne said quickly.

"Rock, rabbit, lizard, shoot." This time, both shot out rocks.

"Best 3 out of 4". Ailne stubbornly claimed.

"Rock, rabbit, lizard, shoot." And this time, both chose lizards.

"Oh this is ridiculous." Ailne huffed, as she went on to state, "Ok, fine, this is the last one for all the marbles."

And with that, they both said "Rock, rabbit, lizard, shoot." Only to look down and see they had both gone back to rabbits.

With a groan, Ailne flung up her paws in disgust. Gray put his paw to his head in disbelief when she started to pace around the room. He saw her start muttering to herself about how only she could get stuck with some boy lirtle with Hercules-like strength to mess up her plans to take on the Hyarks and kill them all.

"Kill them ... how do you plan to kill them?" Gray whispered, almost to himself as he listened to Ailne's muttering. The idea scared him almost more than the idea of facing the Hyarks again since the summer when he had not had time to think about it but had simply grabbed it by its tail (after Lev's roar had shaken the earth like a bomb going off) and thrown the Hyark that was attacking him and his friends off the cliff of

Pangolin Mountain.

"Oh, I don't know, maybe not kill them, but do something close, I mean I am a warrior, it's what my family and I do, we fight and protect. And I need to get them away from the moonflowers in a way that lets me get the moonflowers up to the Batterflies. I need to do something, like kill them, to clear a path so I can get there." Ailne responded to his question but only continued pacing as she continued to mutter about what she planned to do.

"Well, I could help you clear a path? I have done it before; I can grab their tails and throw them really far away. Then it doesn't hurt them too badly either." Gray flexed an arm as if to show his strength but realized that Ailne was just looking at the floor as she wandered the room and did not seem impressed. Gray sheepishly put his arm down.

"There will be too many of them, you will get overwhelmed, that won't work ... well, it may work for a minute, but it won't work for long enough to get the moonflowers there safely to the Batterflies, we need to think of something else." Ailne kept pacing, but it slowed a little as she started to ponder the different options.

Realizing that his suggestions were not being heard and getting tired of watching her pace circles around the room, Gray wandered over to the table to see if there was any of the yummy lirtle drink or food left over that he could eat. Gray realized he was starving since he had eaten his treats long ago, in the first few hours on his first night, and had not eaten since.

While Gray happily helped himself to both the drink and food, Ailne suddenly stood straight up and clapped her paws together.

"I've got it! She exclaimed.

"What do you mean, you've got it?" Gray asked, slightly irritated that Ailne had not even asked for his thoughts or opinion. Gray was a little put off at this point as he just kept thinking about how his plan to help was not being very appreciated. Wasn't he the one that the ancient lirtles had said would come to help Ailne fight the Hyarks, wasn't he the one that was coming to her, and her village's, rescue? He was now so lost in his thoughts about how he was the underdog and unappreciated hero, that he almost tuned out Ailne as she spoke of the plan, but his ears perked up as he caught the end of it as Bunroo's came up in her last sentence of: "... and the Bunroo's will do their part, and that will be that." Ailne finished up excitedly, clearly delighted with her plan.

Unfortunately, while Gray was mentally kicking himself as to why he had not been paying attention sooner to have heard, what, exactly the plan was, as if on cue, there was a knock at the door. Ailne opened it to Baran the Bunroo and three other trusted comrades of his, who all came in at the exact noon sunbeam.

"I have the plan Baran." Ailne said, and again, she started to speak rapidly, and Gray tried to listen in so he would not miss the key details of the quest, as he hated to admit that he had not been paying attention the first time around.

Ailne's paws were whirling as she explained how she thought that if she took the moonflowers in her backpack, and had some of the other lirtles, including Gray, distract the Hyarks at the start, that she could then find a gap to run through. From there, she felt like her tremendous speed would be able to carry her past the dangerous jaws of the Hyarks and across the Highlands to the mountain slopes and the entrance to the cave that led to the Batterflies.

Yet, despite her excitement, Gray could tell that Baran and his colleagues were not happy about the plan. For a second, he thought he heard low toned voices of disapproval from the Bunroos like deep bells, asking Ailne to do something else. Gray thought he heard them say his name.

"Him! You want to take him to the Highlands and get his take on whether my plan will work, are you serious!" Ailne said disgustedly and sat on the bench in a huff – glaring at Gray.

Just then, Saw came through one of the windows and seemed to delight in finding Gray there as he swooped and fluttered around Gray's head before settling comfortably on Gray's shoulder.

"I am happy to see you too Saw." Gray gently stroked the owl with one paw, while he looked at Baran and his friends, as well as Ailne.

"Well, how do we get there?" Gray asked and Ailne snorted. Baran hopped forward and Gray immediately got his answer as Saw flew away and perched on one corner of Baran's pouch.

"Got it." Gray said and as he prepared for another cozy trip in Baran's protective cocoon, he almost laughed when Ailne jumped in first but turned her back to him and refused to say another word.

And with that, upon a gentle roll, the two lirtle children went to see just what they actually would be facing later that night, and how perilous it truly was.

$\mathcal{P}$ART SEVEN – THE PLANS

"How much longer Violet. We need to get going." Lev pulled the blanket around him a little tighter as the wind blew the snow through  the sparse canopy of tree branches and whipped around them.

"I am almost done; I just need a bit more sap for this last balloon and we should have enough." Violet was focused on scraping thick, golden liquid off the trunk of what may have been a maple tree. It was hard to tell what it had been now that they were in the rough land between the villages, where the trees here were weakened by either the harsh wind or beetles that got underneath their bark. To protect themselves, the trees over-produced sap – basically emitting tree blood to try and heal over any broken spots. And Violet was capitalizing on those over-producing trees to gather enough sap to put a good dollop into each of the dozen or more balloon fruit that Holly had brought to them. Lev, Samuel and the gang had been struggling through the driving snow many hours behind Gray, when a Bunroo had appeared suddenly, stepping out of the blizzard like a ghost. It was with relief that Violet, Dawn, and Lev quickly saw the familiar face pop out of the pouch of that Bunroo, letting them know that the Bunroo was a friend and not a foe.

"Holly!!" Dawn greeted their friend. "What are you doing out here?"

"I've come to help you!" Holly replied, as she climbed out of the Bunroo's pouch.

"I realized, once Gray declared to all the other villagers that he had seen a vision in the lunar pools, that you all might have been around or worried. Oh, you should have seen Gray stand up to them – he got so mad before Stelios appeared!" Holly's sing song laugh sung out over across the snow as she tried to make herself look as big as she could before she fell over with a fit of giggles.

"Anyway, I was hiding in a corner, so I think he thought I left, but I heard them all talking, and then I heard the plan but ... well," Holly threw up her hands and wrung them, "I don't think it's a very good one. Gray does not understand how fast or vicious the Hyarks can be, and Ailne won't listen to Gray."

"They need your help, so I thought, if I brought you the balloon fruit, with the sap, you all could somehow figure out, how to get the Hyarks to eat it, and get their teeth all stuck together, to help Gray and Ailne." And with that, Holly was all out of breath, flushed, and stammering.

"Unless, you have a different plan, which I am sure you do, I was just trying to help, and protect them as I don't want them to get hurt."

"Holly – that is a wonderful plan." Samuel chimed in now, and with those words, Holly beamed up at him in adoration. She thought Samuel was the most handsome lirtle she had ever seen, with his green eyes, and golden fur, his long mane that he pulled back in a topknot and him being the oldest in the group by far – he was dreamy.

She blushed a sweet pink from the tip of her head to her toes. Samuel grinned down at the little Pangolin whom he had grown quite fond of in the short time he had known her.

"Okay, well then." Holly squeaked out, "If you have everything, I had better get going. I don't do so well in the snow, my plates get a little frozen, but let me know if things work out okay, I will be back up at Lucky Ledge if needed again."

"Thank you, Holly!" The *Lave* lirtle children and Samuel waved in unison as Holly jumped back into the Bunroo's pouch and then they quickly disappeared into the snowy hills as silently as they had come.

Meanwhile, Gray's stomach felt a little more than queasy as he lay on the side of a hill, looking over and at the Highlands that spread out and blended into the slopes of Pangolin Mountain.

For the last five minutes, Gray and Ailne had been watching the slopes and Ailne had been getting him up to speed on the lay of the land. But it was the most recent "crow" incident that had Gray rolling onto his back and trying not to panic.

Ailne had explained that they were at the southern end of the Highlands and to the east was both her village and even further east was the lush and pretty land of the lirtles, with his village in it and lots of magical spots. To the north was Pangolin Mountain and almost straight ahead, there was a cave at the base of it, which is where she needed to get to, to get the moonflowers to the Batterflies, that lived in the mountain and in its caverns. The Batterflies were the Guardians and saw who was good or bad. And finally, to the west – well, Gray looked to the west and saw the land kind of turn to muddy mire and rocks with long grass. Even with the snow, it was all churned up and brown. The swamplands where the Hyarks lived, before the land turned to ocean. The Hyarks, which looked like hyenas but with great white shark teeth and a hump like fin on their back, had gills and so while they were on land a lot of the time, if they needed to, they could retreat into the water.

And Gray had just witnessed a scary sight. The Highlands were directly in front of them, and just looked a smooth huge field of white snow, with some odd paths in them, the creator of which Gray had only just realized, when a lone crow had been flying over the field and swooped down so it was low to the ground as it flew. Suddenly, from the one end of the field, two humps of fur came up and out of the snow, both heading straight towards the crow with extreme speed. The crow had no chance as two Hyarks barreled up and out of the snow, jaws and rows of teeth snapping, and the crow disappeared with one surprised squawk. It was only a couple of black feathers that floated down after, that let anyone know what had just happened, as the field returned to stillness and eerie silence.

As Gray stared up at the sky, where the clouds and snow had cleared for a brief hour to show him it was the late afternoon and the full moon was coming tonight, he felt that they were doomed. There was no way he could beat the Hyarks – they were too big and too fast. Suddenly, all Gray wanted was his brother Samuel, and his friends – Lev, and Violet and Dawn. They would know what to do.

"See, I told you. He is just a baby – he is not going to help us fight the Hyarks." Ailne said it to the Bunroos, who were all waiting patiently a few feet back.

"I. Am. Not. A. Baby." Gray's doubts were immediately squished, and he rolled back over and stared back at the Highlands to see if he could figure out some way to get past the Hyarks and get to the cave on the other side.

Gray's gaze swept over the full field and upon looking closely, he saw two spots where it seemed possible to get to the base of the mountain and the cave. The first, looked like a series of steps or rock slabs that in the summer, was likely the path most used to go up and down. The other, was a wide swath of a couple dozen feet across where the ground appeared almost bare, with little snow covering it of maybe an inch or two.

"That area over there, why is it so bare?"

Ailne looked at where Gray was pointing and then answered: "That part of the Highlands is on a slight rise, so whenever the wind picks up, it blows the snow off at that point, and it all settles into big drifts. But there is less snow where the actual path is or the stone slabs are, that is where my brother tried to go last time, with two others. He got to the last ledge when seven Hyarks surrounded them, they waited and ambushed them before they attacked, and my brother fought them fiercely, so the other two could escape and come back, but then he disappeared and..." Ailne's voice caught before she whispered, "... and no one has seen him since. There was blood. I believe he fought them off, he is strong and much older than me, a warrior lirtle. But why, if he did succeed, why didn't he come back." She swiped at her cheek, and Gray decided to ignore the tears he saw rolling down.

"Listen, I don't want to go the way your brother went, as you have already seen, it is easy to predict the path and the snow is too deep beside it. I think we should go straight up the middle where there is less snow and it is wide open." Gray stated calmly.

"Are you crazy! That is so dumb – they will eat us alive!" Ailne said in disbelief.

"You have armor, right?" Gray asked. Ailne looked at him quizzically. "I saw that you were wearing silver chainmail armor in the vision when you were talking to Alrik and Stelios, when your parents were begging him not to let you fight." Gray stated simply. "I need armor and anyone who is going to go with us, needs to be wearing armor."

"Who do you want to go with us?" Ailne asked.

"Well, I envision sending out a small army." Gray said calmly, noting that the Bunroos, that had been silently standing by all appeared to be listening intently.

"I think we need to go out in almost a square formation, all the warrior lirtles on the outside, in armor, only the fastest and strongest, then us, and then in the middle we will have the Bunroos. And rather than you or me carrying the moonflowers, although we will make it look like we are with backpacks, one of the Bunroos will actually have the moonflowers hidden in their pouch. It will be our job to protect the Bunroos, or distract the Hyarks, to allow the Bunroos to get close to the mouth of the cave, where they can then scatter, except for the one holding the moonflowers who will go into the cave and deliver the moonflowers to the Batterflies. Once inside the cave, the Hyarks do not dare to go, as the guardians of Rainbow River, if the Hyarks get close or threaten them, their bite while very small is said to be deadly, as it leaves a virus that is incurable. The Batterflies know they are bad."

Gray stopped talking as he had been staring out at the Highlands and the entrance of the cave, remembering the last time he had himself encountered the Batterflies, and shook off a shiver. They had only tested him, not hurt him, he reminded himself. Gray looked back then at the Bunroos and Ailne. The Bunroos were murmuring amongst themselves, deep melodic tones where Gray could not quite hear what they were saying. Nonetheless, Gray did understand when Baran turned and dipped his head in a nod of agreement.

Even Ailne (who wanted to disagree with Gray) could see that the plan made sense. Irritated nonetheless, and still sad thinking about her brother, she finally said, "oh fine, but I get to pick the warriors who are coming, and you have to tell Stelios because I am going to rest until it's dark and time to go." And with that, she marched back over to the Bunroos, but this time she did not get into Baran's pouch. Ailne jumped into another Bunroo's pouch standing to the side, and that

Bunroo took off right after she got in. Since Gray had normally been inside the pouch of any Bunroo that had been moving outside, he only realized then, watching this even taller Bunroo depart with Ailne, that Bunroos had long, powerful hops that he guessed covered at least five feet at a jump. Gray was impressed and realized that his decision to have a Bunroo carry the moonflowers during the mission tonight, was the right one, even as he noted that keeping up with the Bunroos at full speed was going to take all that he, and his little legs, had.

Gray looked over at Baran and swore that Baran shrugged his shoulders in a similar "I don't know what's up with her" fashion, before Gray walked over and realized before climbing in, he had never said it before, though it felt right now, "Thank you Baran."

Again, Baran tipped his head in a nod, and with that, Gray climbed back into Baran's pouch and prepared for the smooth ride back to Ailne's house. Gray hoped to fill Stelios in and rest for a couple of hours before they faced the Hyarks and he tried to finish the task that many other warrior lirtles had apparently failed to do...

Despite the tranquility of the pouch, Gray could not appreciate its peacefulness on the trip back. The weight of the quest and the potential for failure, if not real harm, that would likely occur to others if his plan failed, suddenly started to crush down upon his small shoulders. There would be no

rest for Gray as his mind swirled with details of
what was needed for the battle that night.

$\mathcal{P}$ART EIGHT – THE FULL MOON

The house was again filled to the brim – but this time, the talk was quiet and somber, punctuated only by an occasional clang as metal slid over a head or chainmail swished down over a body. The warriors were all here, hand chosen by Ailne and she had done well.   Tough with manes braided or shorn off, these lirtles were young as well as old – and none of them smiled. Gray gulped after looking into the icy eyes of one warrior, who could not have been much older than him, and was glad they were all on his side.   He also realized that he had not hung around warrior lirtles much, and they were a bit of a different breed, which maybe explained Ailne's attitude and why she had been so prickly.

Musing on that thought as he let the candlelight guide him around the table, Gray thought back on the last hour, as Stelios had in fact come back as the last shreds of sunlight were fading, Gray had filled him in on the plan. Nodding as he listened, Stelios had thought the plan sound and said so. But now, as the evening came on strong, and Gray looked around the room, he second guessed whether he was doing the right thing. The ancient elder's words from only this morning still rang in his ears — about how the village needed to wait for the *Lave* lirtles to come, or the land of the lirtles would be lost. No one else had come, not Lev, or Violet or Dawn, or even his brother Samuel, and now the time had run out, and it was just him and Ailne. Gray worried that they would not be enough.

The others were pre-occupied with their own tasks in preparing. Ever since the viewing on the banks above the Highlands, no one questioned Gray any longer. Whether it was the Bunroos or Ailne, Gray did not know but everyone was respectful in their interactions with him now. Gray was surprised when he saw the loud villager from earlier there, now dressed in chainmail armor and was relieved when the villager just nodded respectfully.

He wandered around, observing the spears and torches that had been prepared and envisioned the scene that would be occurring later. Gray hoped the fire, weapons and fortitude of the pack would be enough to defeat the Hyarks. Gray was happy when Saw flitted in a window and found his shoulder again. It was then that Gray saw Ailne. She was standing near a window, quietly and by herself. Like the first time he saw her in the vision, now in person, she dazzled with her armor and silver blue fur. No, Gray noted to himself, she just sparkled, even in the dark, Ailne was special. He walked up to her, and she looked at him, and then she picked up off the floor the special armor that she had gone specifically to find after the venture out earlier.

It was also a bright silver, and Gray took it carefully from Ailne. Her chin quivered a bit when she said. "It's an extra suit of armor that my brother wore when he was your age. It's the only one I could find in your size. So, don't mess it up."

"I won't. Thank you Ailne." Gray said.

Ailne sniffed before she squared her shoulders and said, "The snow has started again but it seems like the moon will be full shortly, so we had better get going. We need to go to the glen first to get the moonflowers. I also found a backpack like yours to wear to make them think we are taking the moonflowers. I stuffed it with my old blankie that I don't use anymore."

"Well, mine is stuffed with my blankie that I still sleep with every night." Gray said solemnly. Ailne looked up at him then. And they both grinned quick before she hugged her backpack to her chest and then swung it onto her back.

"I knew you were still a baby." She said, but she was smiling, and Gray just smiled back, and let it go this time.

"Okay, let's go and save the land of the lirtles." Gray said, and Ailne said, "Follow me."

...

The group stayed in the house, except for Baran and the other taller Bunroo, who followed

Ailne and Gray once they slipped out a side door. While the Hyarks were supposedly far away near their swamplands, neither Gray nor Ailne wanted to take any chances that somehow, they would discover that the lirtle children were not the ones carrying the moonflowers.

Because it was snowing again, despite it being before midnight, it was bright and light outside. It was easy for Gray to follow Ailne to the magical glen. Then, as the four of them stepped near the moonflowers, the silence and peace filled them all as they gazed upon the beautiful flowers. Carefully, Ailne and Gray plucked the flowers by the stem, and they wrapped them gently in the gossamer silk layers which Stelios had given Gray earlier, that protected the flowers from being crushed.

When they turned to the Bunroos with the moonflowers, Gray had expected Baran to step forward, but it was the taller Bunroo that did so. Gray looked quizzically at Baran but Ailne responded to his unspoken question.

"This is Bjorn, Baran's brother, and he will take the moonflowers because they are both worried that Baran has a family, and since you met Baran's youngest son, Bastian, you can understand that Baran needs to be okay to return to his family again. He can't run the risk by bearing the moonflowers to the Batterflies."

"Oh, yes I understand that." It was all Gray

could say as again, the weight and fear hit him that after tonight, some of the villagers, those who put their trust and faith in him, may not be returning to their families or loved ones in the morning. Understanding Gray's conflict, Baran put a paw on his shoulder and pulled him close, where Gray buried his face in the soft fur and took some comfort for a second.

Suddenly, Saw burst into the glen, and started flittering around them all, breaking the quiet with his hoots.

"Okay Saw. Let's go." Gray pushed away from Baran and prepared to lead everyone onto what felt was a battle ground. Gray made the decision then, that he would not let them down.

...

The snow crunched under their feet as the group reached the edge of the wide gap that would mark the start of the gauntlet, or race across the Highlands towards the cave. Gray had gone over the plan with the whole group, so each knew their role, and knew whom they were protecting. If the Hyarks started to separate or overwhelm them, they had strict instructions to save themselves and get back to the banks where it was safe, or to head home. On the command of Gray, whom was near the back of the formation but slightly inside it, the warriors were to light the torches and the whole procession would start running. As soon as the Hyarks started attacking, the goal was to fight with fire, spears, and Gray's strength to let Ailne and the Bunroos stay at the front with Ailne appearing to be the one carrying the moonflowers. Near the end, Ailne would jump into Baran's pouch, hopefully as he and Bjorn made it to the end of the gauntlet, and Baran would peel off to the slopes and protections offered in the trees of the mountain before looping back around. Gray prayed that Bjorn would make it unharmed, or that somehow the Batterflies would help protect him because the Bunroos had no weapons besides their speed and incredibly powerful hind legs.

Gray had his paw raised, and the warriors with the torches lit them up. The night felt like it became ablaze as flames and smoke started to light the sky. As Gray went to drop his paw, the sign to start, suddenly the air was filled with the blood curdling screaming yips of a dozen or more Hyarks in the near vicinity. Gray had to steady himself as he started to shake and told himself to stay brave, to stay strong – like his brother Samuel would be.

"3, 2, 1, go!" Gray dropped his paw and the group started racing across the land, just as the snow stopped falling. The land shook as they passed over, and the screaming howls of the Hyarks became frenzied as they caught scent of the group. It felt like it was only a second or two, before the Hyarks burst out of the snow drifts, snarling monsters as their red eyes reflected the flames and they ran at the group without caution to the flames or spears. Snarls and whimpers charged the air as one Hyark ran straight into several spears, and another got too close to a torch. The smell of burning hair and flesh filled Gray's nose. Gray was still running as fast as he could, and his lungs felt like they were going to explode as he tried to keep up with the agile Bunroos just ahead of him. But Gray was starting to lag from the group, and he could smell, as well as feel the hot, stinking breath of a Hyark hunting him down, as it gnashed its teeth behind him. The other warriors did not notice Gray starting to lag as they were all fighting for their lives with attacks coming from every direction. Just as Gray felt the Hyark was getting ready to jump and catch him, Gray stumbled and fell to his knee, where the Hyark was in mid-air and went over him.

With flash backs of the night up high on the mountain, Gray saw his chance to grab the Hyark that was now in front of him, by his leg, and with the strength that he only recently knew he possessed, Gray stood and flung the Hyark high into the air and away, where it flew through the night and fell somewhere into the snow banks a way away. Back on his feet, Gray saw the group was slowing and only about ten feet ahead of him as the fighting became more intense. A few of the warriors were being drawn away from protecting the Bunroos and the Hyarks were separating them. Gray started running as he saw a Hyark, with jaws open wide, about to attack a warrior, when suddenly, whizzing through the air, a ball bulleted past Gray's ear, into the Hyark's jaws. It snapped its jaws closed in surprise and when it tried to open them, it started to growl in confusion as a thick golden substance started oozing through its teeth, slowly sealing them shut with every bite it attempted to take. Shaking its head, the Hyark stopped moving as it attempted to dislodge the substance.   Then, more balls whizzed past Gray, and two more Hyarks met the same fate. Gray looked up and two his surprise, he saw back, probably fifty feet or so, Samuel and Dawn, with slingshots aimed, firing balloon fruit into the mouths of the Hyarks and stopping them in their tracks.

"You came – the *Lave* lirtles came!" It was all Gray could say before he had to roll out of the way as a huge Hyark loomed over him. But this Hyark, an ugly scarred creature, was not looking at him, he was looking only at Ailne who was still running at the front with Baran and Bjorn. "Nooo." Gray yelled, just as the Hyark lunged past him and raced towards its targets. A ball whizzed towards the creature, but just hit its neck, exploding as it did. Gray could not catch it. The group was past the halfway mark, and some of the warriors were having to retreat as the Hyarks separated them from the rest of the group and threatened to ambush them.

In horror, Gray watched as the Hyark's strides ate up the ground before it tensed and then lunged with one huge stride, jaws outstretched and intending to snap down upon Ailne who was a blur as she raced with the Bunroos up the last rise of the mountain. But just as his jaws seemed about to close on her – Gray saw a tiny blob of brown attack the side of its face as little claws drove into its left eye. Screaming in pain, the Hyark turned its head and bit down on the wing of Saw, who was valiantly defending Ailne, before flinging the owl twenty feet into the snow like a little rag doll.

Although only a few seconds, the temporary diversion gave Baran enough time to scoop Ailne off and they were peeling away and already disappearing into the outskirts of the trees by the time the huge Hyark regained its bearings and now zeroed in on Bjorn who was almost to the cave, but not there yet. Howling in rage, the Hyark took off and the other Hyarks followed suit. Just then, a growl like a bomb went off, and Gray cheered even as it layed him on the ground too like everyone else, because he knew Lev was trying to slow the Hyarks down. Bjorn the Bunroo, fortunately, was able to stay up and keep going, albeit not as fast. The other Hyarks that were stunned, Gray ran to and threw them by legs or tails, whatever he could grab from behind or surprise, where he had thrown five or six into the banks thirty or forty feet away before they regained their balance. There were still a couple warriors with torches and spears that were helping ward off any remaining Hyarks. Lev and the gang were shooting the balls of balloon fruit into any open mouths, effectively causing the Hyarks to lock their own jaws together like a steel trap as the tree sap worked into their teeth.

But Gray again felt dismay as he saw the leader, the huge Hyark still going after Bjorn, where while Bjorn was back to racing, the Hyark was making up ground. Gray suddenly felt sick as he realized that Bjorn was not going to make it. With thirty, then twenty, then ten feet, the Hyark was running Bjorn down, yet just as Gray thought that Bjorn was going to be caught, silver and black creatures poured out of the mouth of the cave. The Batterflies were silent and deadly as they flew past Bjorn and homed in on the Hyark. They darted down and to any one just observing, it looked like they only landed for a second on the Hyark, but from the way the Hyark's body sagged, and the sound that came out of its throat, was of a whimpering pain that seemed unbearable. Gray knew that the Hyark had probably been bitten a dozen or more times.

It stopped the Hyark in its tracks. As the Hyark moaned and started to drag itself back and away from the mouth of the cave, the other Hyarks saw their fallen leader, and they instinctively knew that they had lost. They started yipping and howling as they gathered around the injured Hyark. They slowly moved together with it, until they disappeared into the snowbanks, without so much as looking back at the lirtles left in the middle of the field.

Gray was still standing, just standing, in the middle of the area for minutes after the Hyarks disappeared back into the snow. Not really doing or seeing anything, when Lev, Dawn and Violet appeared by his side. It was when Samuel grabbed Gray in a huge bear hug, that Gray just started bawling as his emotions overwhelmed him.

"It's okay Gray. Look Gray – look up, you did it." Samuel whispered to his little brother, and the group all looked up to the entrance of the cave where Bjorn now stood, waving, and he was surrounded by Batterflies. But this time, the warm glow that came from the Batterflies' wings, shone brilliantly out across the Highlands in the most beautiful pastel colors one could imagine.

"They are saying thank you Gray. You got the moonflowers to them. They can now hibernate with the moonflowers despite the early snowfall and will live to pollenate everything in the spring. You saved the land of the lirtles – Gray you did it." Dawn was speaking now in her knowing and wise way.

"I did not do it, I did not, you and the others did. And Saw, Saw's hurt. Lev, I am so sorry. I could not protect Saw, and I don't know where he is but I saw him flung by his wing. I am so sorry Lev – Saw is your pet, and I didn't save him." Gray was sobbing as guilt swept over him.

"It's okay Gray, we got here right before that happened and we were there to see Saw get flung but we have all been searching over there, and Saw isn't there. We think he must be okay, or he is hiding until he thinks it's safe and then he will come back. He may have a broken wing, but Saw is tough, he will be okay. I can feel it." Dawn again was speaking, reassuring Gray until he stopped crying and was just hiccupping a bit.

"Well, okay, I guess." Gray finally felt like things were starting to be a little bit better once the shock and the adrenaline of the fight were wearing off. "Are the others, okay?" He asked.

"Yes, everyone else is okay, a few cuts and one nasty bite to a leg, but no one else got hurt and you did it. Ailne is back at her house with Baran, and we should go back there, you should rest." Violet now chimed in.

"I think that would be a good idea." Gray said, "You should meet some of my new friends, and the Bunroos, they are great." Gray was almost delirious, and he did not even realize when Samuel swung him up and gave him a piggyback all the way to the house, because he was so tired. Gray babbled to them until they got to Ailne's house, where he saw Ailne and gave her a quick hug. Her parents were there, and her mother, weeping, gave Gray an embrace and kissed him on the cheek. She thanked him for protecting their daughter and saving their village. And then, Gray finally was put into an extra bed, where he passed out into a deep sleep, and finally, in sleep, a tiny smile touched his lips as he snuggled with his blankie.

...

The following morning, Gray felt warm sunlight on his face, and it took a second for him to remember where he was. Realizing he was in Ailne's home, his eyes were still closed, and he groaned a little bit as he stretched under the soft blankets. As he tested out his limbs, he realized he was okay but just a little beat up. He opened his eyes and saw the kind brown ones of Stelios looking down on him. Stelios was smiling at him, and Gray was more than happy to smile back. "I am so proud of you Gray, you did it. You saved the land of the lirtles." Stelios told him.

For a second, Gray felt like his heart was going to burst out of his chest, as he was so happy to hear that. But then, he remembered about Saw, and he felt sorrow about to take over. Gulping back the tears that were bubbling up from his throat, Gray went to ask Stelios about Saw, when Gray's mouth formed an "o" in shock. Stelios was sitting and was stroking Gray's face with one wing, but the other was wrapped in a sling of strips and salve .... The wrapping appeared very similar to the one that Holly had put on Gray's ankle after he had gotten bitten by the Foxfish. Moreover, the way Stelios was cradling it, his wing seemed broken.

Stelios watched Gray's face and saw all of the emotions, the questions, and the puzzled expressions go through his lovely smoke colored eyes, before suddenly Gray went totally relaxed and he leaned back on the bed, almost joyfully, finally at ease for the first time in three days.

As Gray's eyes closed again, all Gray murmured as he drifted back to sleep, and which made Stelios' lips twitch into a grin, was, "I'm so glad that Saw is okay."

The End.

About The Author:

Julia D. Kyte is the author of the popular *Lirtle* series. In addition to writing fantasy novels in her spare time, she is a litigation lawyer and co-owner/coach at CrossFit Helo. Born and raised in British Columbia, Canada, Julia currently resides just outside of Salt Lake City, Utah, with her husband and two boys.

Author Photo Credit: Kristin Louise Photography